AND IT IS STILL THAT WAY

Legends told by
Arizona Indian Children

collected by

BYRD BAYLOR

TRAILS WEST PUBLISHING

Library of Congress Cataloging in Publication Data

Main entry under title:
And it is still that way.

SUMMARY: American Indian Children retell forty
tribal legends in contemporary language.

1. Indians of North America — Arizona — Legends.
[1. Indians of North America — Legends] I. Baylor, Byrd.
E78.A7A65   398.2'452'09791 [398.2]   76-42242
ISBN 0-939729-06-7

Illustrations & Design by
Lucy Jelinek

ACKNOWLEDGMENTS

I want to share the names of friends who gave me special help in gathering these stories and made the project such a happy one.

Vernon Masayesva, Jon Cordalis, and Brian Honyauti at the Hotevilla-Bacabi Community School, Third Mesa, Hopi Reservation

Robert K. Caldwell, Walter Koyawena, and Ethel Kane at Second Mesa Day School, Second Mesa, Hopi Reservation

Nancy Chase Huotari and Carlos Salas at Rice Elementary School at San Carlos, San Carlos Apache Reservation

Martha Ahern at Arizona Western Institute of Consumer Education at Yuma

Barbara Antone at the Ft. Yuma Community Library, Yuma

Kathryn Michel at Carlisle School (C.I.T.E. Program), Somerton

Arlene Jorgensen, Melveta Walker, and Patty Worth at the Tuba City Boarding School, Tuba City, Navajo Reservation

Sister Francella and Sister Patrice at St. John's School, St. John's Mission, Laveen

Sister Estelle at Topawa School, Topawa Village, Papago Reservation

Tally Gilkerson with the Tucson Public Library programs on the Papago Reservation

Mary A. Smith, Phoenix Indian School, Phoenix

CONTENTS

People Can Turn into Anything 41

Brother Coyote 51

There Is Magic All Around Us 73

INTRODUCTION

Arizona Indian children made this book themselves, every word of it, every page.

It happened because I stopped one day at the small Papago village of Topawa, far out in the dry hot cactus desert of southern Arizona where I live. Somebody had told me the children in the school there were writing down Papago legends, and I wanted to see them. No special reason, I thought. I just like Indian legends and I'd never read any written by children.

Tacked up on the wall of the schoolroom, with a picture for every page, was a story about Rattlesnake and how he made the first brush shelter (we use the Spanish word *ramada*) so the Papago people would have shade. You'd almost have to squint up at our fierce bright sun to know why they needed that first shade so much.

As soon as I read the story, I knew I wanted a special kind of book to hold this special kind of story. It would have to be written by children, not tampered with too much by adults.

So I took the Rattlesnake story with me for good luck and camped in my favorite places and went to dances and ceremonials along the way . . . and talked to children in reservation schools.

We talked about storytelling in the Indian way. We talked about how it feels to hear stories that aren't made up new and written down in somebody else's book but are as old as your tribe and are told and sung and chanted by people of your own family, your own clan.

We talked about how it feels to hear stories that go back to the oldest memories of your ancestors, to times when animals talked like people, times when people changed into stars or rocks or eagles, times when the world was still new and there were monsters to be killed and heroes to kill them and gods to teach the first people the first things they needed to know.

I asked the children — Navajo, Hopi, Papago, Pima, Apache, Quechan, Cocopah — to choose a story told to them by someone in their own tribe. It should be their favorite story, I said, maybe the best story in the world. Some children offered to write, others wanted to draw pictures. This would be their gift to other tribes, to other children. It would be sharing some of the oldest magic of the Indian world.

Here in Arizona, Indians don't tell their stories in summer. The old people say snakes don't like to hear them and sometimes it makes them angry and they come and bite the storyteller. So stories are saved for winter when the snakes are sleeping.

In gathering these stories, I saved them for winter too. I did not ask anyone to tell them in summer and I hope whoever reads them now will put the book away during the hot part of the year when snakes are listening.

If you read these stories aloud in winter you will know that somewhere in Arizona your Indian sisters, your Indian brothers, are hearing them too. Wherever they live, in some Navajo *hogan* or some Apache *wickiup*, a storyteller is speaking. On some high rocky Hopi *mesa* or down in the sandy Pima desert by a campfire people sit close together listening still.

Most of these stories are just bits and pieces of longer and more complicated legends, but they are the part children remember.

Indians know that in nature, things go in fours. In Indian magic, things go in fours. You will notice in these stories that the number *four* has special power. In fact, many of the original stories take four nights to tell.

Indians say no one is supposed to fall asleep while a storyteller is speaking. In the old days even the littlest children had to pay attention to every word or the storyteller would stop. So it used to be that whenever he would pause every person would quickly make some sign that he was listening. The Papagos always repeated the last word they had heard. The Hopis answered with a soft Hopi sound, barely louder than a breath. Each tribe had its own way of saying to the storyteller, "I am listening. Go on."

When Indian legends are told today, they never end with the feeling that they are something out of the past and finished. Instead, the storyteller will probably say, "It can happen like that now," or "We still know such things," or "And it is still that way."

So everything that went before still touches us. You can tell that in these stories.

Byrd Baylor

WHY ANIMALS ARE THE WAY THEY ARE

Animals have a special place in these stories because the Indians feel close to them. They know that animals were on the earth before people were created and that animals know many secrets about life people still don't know.

WHY DOGS
DON'T TALK
ANYMORE

Old Quechan people have a favorite story that they tell to Quechan children.

They say dogs used to talk just like people. They spoke in Indian language and said anything they wanted.

Dogs lived among their Indian masters and talked all the time. The only trouble was that the dogs talked too much. They never stopped. Whenever anything happened—they told it. Whatever they heard—they told it. Whatever they saw—they told it.

No one could keep a secret. No one could hide anything. The dogs told everything. It was terrible.

The Indians got together and asked the Great Spirit: "O Great Spirit, hear our prayer. Do something about these dogs of ours. We cannot keep a secret anymore."

But the dogs went on telling this and that. Each night the people went to bed wondering what new secrets the dogs would be telling when they woke up.

One morning an old man stood up and shoved his dog.

"Well, dog," he said, "go tell everybody I shoved you."

The dog just looked at him for a minute. He said nothing.

The old man was surprised. He tried something else. He whispered a secret.

Then he said, "Well, dog, go ahead and tell everybody my secret."

Again, the dog just looked at him. He didn't say a word. He didn't tell the secret.

Instead, he BARKED. He only barked.

What a relief! The Indian people knew that the Great Spirit had found a way to answer their prayers.

When they tell it now, Quechan Indians always say that it is true dogs could once talk. But they didn't use their talking for a good cause. That's why it was taken away from them.

Now dogs bark a lot. Whenever they see a person coming into an Indian village they bark. When they hear a sound at night they bark. They always bark—but they don't tell secrets anymore.

So you better be careful how you use your talking. You might end up just having to bark.

Group story: Quechan, Ft. Yuma Library

WHY RATTLESNAKE
HAS FANGS

Rattlesnake used to be the gentlest little animal. The Sun God forgot to give Rattlesnake a weapon to protect himself and he was called Soft Child.

The animals liked to hear him rattle so they teased him all the time. One day at a ceremonial dance a mean little rabbit said, "Let's have some fun with Soft Child."

He started to throw poor helpless little Rattlesnake around.

"Catch," yelled Skunk as he threw Soft Child back to Rabbit.

They had a good time but Rattlesnake was unhappy and there was nothing he could do about it.

The Sun God felt sorry for the sad little snake and he told him what to do.

"Get two sharp thorns from the devil's claw plant and put them in your mouth."

Rattlesnake picked the devil's claw and put the thorns in his upper jaw.

"Now you will have to rattle to give a warning. Strike only if you have to." That is what the Sun God told him.

The next day Rabbit began to kick the snake and throw him around the way he always did.

Rattlesnake began to rattle his warning but Rabbit just laughed and kicked him again. Soft Child remembered the thorns he held in his mouth. He used them on Rabbit.

After that every animal backed away from Rattlesnake and he was not called Soft Child any longer.

To this day, Rattlesnake only strikes if he has to but everyone fears him.

Cheryl Giff ● Pima, St. John's School

WHY COYOTE
ISN'T BLUE

Long before other people were made, Coyote was walking around on the earth. He saw two bluebirds swimming in a pond. They seemed to be singing a certain song he had not heard before.

"What are you doing?" he asked them.

"We are renewing our feathers. We are keeping them blue."

Coyote wanted to be blue too. He asked them if he could make himself blue the way they did.

The birds told him the way to do it. "You swim in this pond four times every morning for four days. And every morning you sing this certain magic song."

"Teach me the song," Coyote said.

The bluebirds taught Coyote the song but they warned him that everything had to be done in the proper order to make it work.

Of course Coyote didn't listen to them. After he knew the song very well he jumped into the water and swam to the other side. He only did it once. He climbed out.

His brown fur was already blue and that made him very happy. He did not wait for the four days to pass. He just started singing the song as he ran off across the hills.

The birds saw that he was not following the rules of the color-changing ceremony. They flew after him at first and tried to get him to come back and swim four times.

Coyote didn't listen to them. He was already blue so he didn't care what they said. He was so proud of himself that he wanted all the animals to see him, so he sang louder and louder as he ran along.

Since there was no one else to see him, he kept looking at himself. He was not watching the path at all, just admiring his blue fur. He tripped over a rock and fell to the ground and rolled over and over in the soft dirt.

When Coyote got up again his fur was the color of dirt...just like it is today.

If only Coyote had listened to the birds he would be blue today.

Noel Roubidoux ● Pima, St. John's School

WHY BEARS
HAVE
SHORT TAILS

Fox was fishing in the river. When he had ten fish he put them on his back and walked off into the woods.

Bear came along and saw Fox with the fish on his back.

"How come you have so many fishes on your back? How are you fishing those fishes out of the water?"

Fox said. "It's easy. You sit on the ice and put your tail in the river. The fishes catch onto your tail and when you get up there will be all of those fishes just hanging on."

"Thanks," said Bear as he ran off toward the river.

He didn't know Fox was laughing as he went along through the woods with his ten fish.

Bear sat on the ice. He sat there a long time, waiting and waiting. He didn't notice any fish jumping onto his tail. All he noticed was that his tail was freezing. It hurt.

After a long time, Bear said, "I can't feel my tail."

He got up and looked. It was true. His long tail had frozen off. All he had left was a very short tail.

Bear was angry. He gave up fishing and ran into the woods looking for Fox.

Fox was cooking his ten fish when Bear grabbed him.

Bear said, "You tricked me and my beautiful long tail froze off. So now I'm taking you back to that river. I'll throw you in and let you freeze."

"No," Fox said. "Don't do that. If you let me go I'll give you all my fish."

So Bear let Fox go and ate all the fish himself and warmed his short tail by Fox's fire.

Now all bears have short tails. This is how it happened.

Sandra Begay • Navajo, Tuba City Boarding School

WHY DOGS
SNIFF

This is one of the first stories I heard. My grandfather told it when I was four years old.

The dogs from our village gathered in the cornfield to have a dance. Every dog around came to join his friends.

They took off their tails and hung them up on the leaves of the corn plants. They were dancing that way when they heard a noise coming from the other side of the field. The noise frightened them so they ran and grabbed any tail they could find and hurried back to the village.

That is why dogs still go around sniffing at each other's tails. They want their own tails back.

Ann Vavages • Pima, Phoenix Indian School

WHY OUR WORLD IS LIKE IT IS

> It is a good feeling to know that the center of the world is where your people live, that the mountains you see every day are sacred places where the spirits stay, that the familiar close-up things are also the sacred things.

HOW THE PAPAGOS
GOT SOME
SHADE

Rattlesnake was a powerful medicine man. But even so he became very sick. His wife did everything she could for him but Rattlesnake did not get any better. He was dying.

He called his best friends, Jackrabbit, Turtle, and Coyote.

He told them, "Make me a place where I can lie until I die. I will lie on the west side in the morning and on the east side in the afternoon."

That is what he said.

His friends didn't know what kind of place he wanted. So they just dug a hole. That seemed like a good house to them.

Then they went to take Rattlesnake to his new house. Rattlesnake was disappointed but he did not let his friends know it.

IIe said, "It is a nice hole and you can put me in it when I die. But now make me a house like I told you."

His friends thought Rattlesnake did not know what he was saying because he was so sick. So they put up a windbreak.

But Rattlesnake did not want a windbreak. He wanted a place that would be open but would have shade on the west side in the morning and shade on the east side in the afternoon.

When Rattlesnake saw the windbreak he said, "This kind of house is good to stop the wind but it is not what I want."

What he wanted was a brush shelter. In Papago language today we call it *watto* or *ramada*, but in those days there was not a brush shelter anywhere around. No one had ever thought of building anything that way. So Rattlesnake's friends did not understand what he wanted. They quickly put up a real house.

"It's a nice house for my wife to live in after I die but it is not what I want now."

Jackrabbit and Turtle and Coyote couldn't figure out what their friend wanted.

Finally Rattlesnake told them, "Make me one that is covered like a house. The roof can be made with brush and there should be four posts to hold it up, but there should not be any walls. When the shade moves, I'll move with it."

His friends then knew what he wanted. They built the first watto and Rattlesnake died in its shade.

They buried him in the hole they had dug.

His wife moved into the house near the windbreak.

And all the Papago people use wattos for shade to this day.

Group story: Papago, Topawa School

HOW OUR PEOPLE
CAME TO BE

In the first days of the world there were no people. The maker of the world wanted people walking around the desert and he wanted them to be a beautiful brown color so he made them out of sand and water.

Out of little bits of mud he shaped the first people. They were the Cocopah and Maricopa and Quechan Indians. He told them they could have the desert to live in and he showed them everything they would need to know to get along in a hot dry place. He taught them what plants to eat and what ceremonies to do to make rain come.

This maker of the world was called KWIKUMAT. He had special colors of his own — red and black. He told the people to remember that red was for blood because blood gives life and that black was for the darkness that means death.

To thank him for making us, we use those same colors now in the special clothes we wear for ceremonies. And we keep this design of KWIKUMAT in our tribe. It is supposed to remind us of how we started and it also reminds us that life and death are part of every person. They go together.

Group story: Quechan, Ft. Yuma Library

WHY NAVAJOS
LIVE IN
HOGANS

We like *hogans* better than houses. This is because of something that happened when the First People came up from the underworld.

They could not find any shelter and they did not know where they were going to live. While they were walking about the earth looking for a home, a spirit spoke to them. They could not see this spirit but they heard a voice saying that two hogans were waiting for them. First Man and First Woman followed that voice to the place where the hogans stood.

They saw that the hogans faced east and had an opening toward the rising sun. They were very beautiful. The voice told them that the hogans had to be blessed before anyone could live in them.

That day Talking God made the first blessing ceremony and First Man and First Woman watched.

One of the hogans was round and it was called a female hogan. The other one was the forked kind and it was called a male hogan.

The male hogan was blessed with many songs and prayers and with white corn. The female hogan was blessed with many songs and prayers and with yellow corn. Then they were ready for First People to live in.

That is how Navajos learned what kind of blessing makes a home safe and brings good luck and happiness and food and children to the people who live there.

Even now a hogan must face the east and must be blessed and sung over in the way First Man and First Woman learned.

Matilda Skacy • Navajo, Tuba City Boarding School

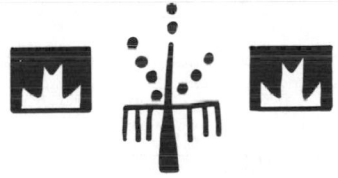

WHY WE HAVE
DOGS IN
HOPI VILLAGES

There was a boy about our age. He lived in a Hopi village way up on the *mesa*. In those days the people were always arguing and fussing with each other and this boy used to say he was going to find some way to stop all that bad feeling.

He thought that if he went away and saw another village where people got along better he could come back and tell his people what to do and they would thank him.

He knew it would be a long journey. But all he took with him was a water jar and a loaf of bread that his mother baked for him.

When he went down the path that led away from his village he did not know which way to go. He just walked where he felt like going. Day after day he walked.

After many days had passed the boy came to the edge of a village he had never seen. It seemed like a happy place where people got along. But as he came closer he could see that it was a village of dogs, not people.

He asked the dogs if he could speak to their chief. Even though they had never seen a human before, they could tell that this boy came in peace so they let him enter their village.

They took him down the ladder into the *kiva* where councils and ceremonies are held. The dog chief sat with all his dog councilmen in a circle. The boy joined them in the circle. They all smoked the peace pipe together. Everyone took four puffs and passed the pipe around four times, right and left. The boy smoked with them.

Then it was time to speak. The boy said, "I came to get your help so the people of my village can find out how to stop arguing and fighting all the time. Maybe some of those dogs will go back with me."

But the chief said, "It will be up to my people. I will have no part in this."

They came out of the kiva together but none of the dogs offered to go with the boy. None of them wanted to leave his own village.

When night came the boy went to a little clearing outside the village and he lay awake for a long time trying to think of a way to get the dogs to go with him.

At last a spirit came down to him from the North Star.

"What do you want?" the spirit asked. "I have all the things that you could want."

The boy did not know what to ask for. But he remembered that many of the dogs looked thin and hungry so he said, "Some food would be good."

The spirit got the food and blessed it. When the boy awoke the food was there beside him. Some of the dogs ran up to the pile of food and began to eat it.

As soon as the boy saw that the dogs were eating the blessed food he knew he had asked the spirit for the right thing. He knew he had found a way to make the dogs follow him.

He went down into the kiva again with the dog leaders of the village. Again they puffed the peace pipe four times each and again the pipe went around four times, right and left.

Then the boy told the chief, "Some of the dogs ate my food. Those are the dogs that will be willing to go with me. They belong to me now because they took my food."

It was true.

The dogs that had eaten the blessed food gathered around the boy wherever he stood. They followed him all the way to his own village up on the mesa.

He gave one dog to each family. The people were so happy to have the dogs that they stopped quarreling.

Hopi villages have been peaceful ever since.

Now dogs have their jobs here. They guard our houses and our people and go to the fields with us and watch over the sheep. And they still remind us not to quarrel. That is their main job.

Group story: Hopi, Second Mesa Day School

THE FOURTH WORLD
OF THE HOPIS

The Hopi people came up from a hole in the ground. When they die they go back into the hole to another world.

The first world of the Hopi Indians was a bad place. The god who made the world said he would make a second world. He told Spider Woman that she should lead the people to the second world.

She showed them the way and when they got there they started planting and building homes but things were not good. There was a lot of killing going on and there was no game to hunt.

Spider Woman went to the god and told him what was happening. He said he would make a third world and that Spider Woman should lead the people again.

In the third world there was no killing and for a while there was enough game. The people tried to plant food but the plants could not grow because there was no light and no heat.

The god told Spider Woman to build bonfires around the field. The fire gave some heat and light and the people built fires every day. That way they were able to make things grow. But still that dark world was not good. People were dying. Again Spider Woman went to tell the god what was happening.

He said he would make the fourth world. It would be the last one he was going to make, he said.

The Hopi people started on the long journey to the fourth world. It took a long time to get there but at last the people came up into the light. They found good land to plant.

They lived high up on the *mesas* where they were safe from their enemies, the Navajos and Utes and other tribes.

Now there are roads leading up to the thirteen Hopi villages, the same roads that used to be trails made by the first Hopis. The Hopis still have the same shrines as their ancestors had.

The Hopi people have a good life. They grow their crops in peace. The men make *kachina* dolls out of cottonwood and the women make baskets out of yucca and pottery out of clay.

The Hopis are still in the fourth world. They thank the god and Spider Woman by taking prayer feathers to the shrines.

The Hopis enjoy staying in the fourth world.

Reynold Nash ● Hopi, Phoenix Indian School

WHY SAGUAROS GROW
ON THE SOUTH SIDE
OF HILLS

The world had just been made. Coyote was supposed to be helping Elder Brother plant seeds and he was walking around the empty desert with his paw closed.

Another coyote came up to him and said, "Open your hand, brother. I want to see what you have there."

He opened his hand. It was full of seeds for saguaro cactus. The other coyote hit his hand and the seeds were scattered right where they were—on the south side of a hill.

That is why even now you see saguaros growing mostly on the south side of the hills. The seeds remember where Coyote threw them.

Robert Juan • Pima-Papago, Ft. Yuma Library

WHY BIRDS
LIVE IN
OUR VILLAGES

The Hano people lived on a high, flat *mesa* at the top of the cliff. Birds flew over to the Hano village looking for anything they could find to eat in the trash and ashes. They would search for food and then fly back to a hill north of the village where they lived.

One day the bird chief went to the village chief to talk about food.

"Look," the bird chief said, "we have to come all the way over here to find food. It's a long way to come."

The two chiefs smoked together the way chiefs do.

The bird chief said to the village chief, "We cannot understand you when you talk."

The Hano chief said, "You should know our language by now. You sit on the roofs of our houses and listen to our words."

They looked around and they could see that some of the birds were resting on the roofs of the houses.

The Hano chief told the bird chief, "Go back and tell the birds they are welcome to come and live right here with us. There is food enough for the birds and the Hanos both."

That is why you see so many birds in our villages today. They live so close they understand our language.

Danny Joseph ● Hopi, Second Mesa Day School

HOW OCEANS CAME TO BE

I'itoi, a Great Spirit of the Papago tribe, knew everything before it happened.

He knew that a flood was going to come and cover the earth, so he wove himself a big watertight basket. He sat in it and floated around during the flood.

After the flood was over, he noticed that the earth was still floating in water. It could not settle in one place.

I'itoi knew what to do. He called the spiders to come and weave webs to hold the land steady. He told them to sew earth and sky together. The spiders worked as hard as they could, but in some places the webs were not strong enough to hold back the water.

Those places can still be seen. They are the lakes and oceans.

Dianne Orosco • Papago, Phoenix Indian School

GREAT TROUBLES AND GREAT HEROES

All people everywhere have heroes that they remember.

But a Hopi girl told me one day, "I know a lot of those stories about heroes. I didn't write them down for you, though, because kachinas are better and you can see them right there in the plaza tomorrow."

THE
BRAVE
MOUSE

Long ago at Old Oraibi there was a chicken hawk that killed almost all the chickens in the village. He was eating them one by one. Finally there were almost no chickens left.

Nobody in the village could kill that hawk. They talked about it down in the *kiva* where a little mouse happened to be listening. He heard the bad news.

This mouse wanted to help the people of his village. He made a plan.

First he cut a hole in the top of the kiva. Then he whittled a very sharp point on one end of a stick. He put that stick through the hole. Next, he went outside himself and sat on top of the kiva very close to the sharp stick.

He knew the hawk would see a tiny mouse and come diving down from the sky to get him. Even though he was afraid, the mouse sat there waiting.

Finally the hawk saw the mouse and came flying toward him. The mouse did not move until the hawk was almost on him. Then he jumped away and the hawk flew into the sharp stick and was killed.

The people were so happy everybody brought the mouse something good to eat.

Donita Lomatska • Hopi, Phoenix Indian School

EAGLEMAN

There was a man who had magic power in gambling. He would cheat and lie and he used his power to win in a certain gambling game that he played every day.

He wanted the daughter of the medicine man, but the medicine man did not want his daughter to marry him. So the medicine man decided to use his power to get rid of him.

He took some feathers from the nest of a large bird and ground them into powder. He told his daughter to sing to the feathers. Then he mixed the feathers into a bowl of thick, good-tasting *pinole*.

There was a pond near where the medicine man and his daughter lived, and every day the gambler used to stop by the pond for a drink of water before he went looking for someone to gamble with. The medicine man told his daughter to take the bowl of pinole to the pond and give it to the gambler when he came by that morning.

The girl did what her father told her. As soon as she handed the man the pinole he drank it down.

The second it was in his mouth he started to shake. Goose bumps covered his body. Eagle feathers began to grow on him and his arms turned into huge eagle wings.

When the people of the village ran to look at him, he flew away. When people shot arrows at him he grabbed those arrows in his claws.

Now his name was Eagleman.

Eagleman flew south past the village that had been the medicine man's home. Near there he found a high mountain (which is now called Baboquívari) and up on the highest cliff of that mountain he found a lonely cave to live in.

Eagleman was so large he needed a lot of food. He would swoop down over the village and catch people and carry them up to his cave and eat them. He needed one person to eat every day.

One day he captured the girl who had given him the pinole. He carried her up to his cave and made her live there with him. She knew she could not climb down and she thought no one in the world could climb up there to save her.

The people of the village knew Eagleman must be killed or no people would be left. Eagleman was eating them so fast there were only a few left to try to carry on the life of the village. They were helpless when Eagleman flew down toward them.

The medicine man who had turned Eagleman into an eagle was not powerful enough to kill him. Finally the people made a trip to the mountain where Se-eh-ha lived. Se-eh-ha, who is also called Elder Brother, is the most powerful medicine man anywhere because he is the one who made the world.

Se-eh-ha could change form whenever he wanted to. The day the people went to him, he was a small old man, bent over.

When they told him that if he did not save his people they would all die, he agreed to go to Eagleman's cave in four days. He gave them seeds to plant at the foot of the mountain where Eagleman lived. In four days a giant gourd vine grew up there, tall enough for Se-eh-ha to climb.

The little old man had a hard climb up the steep cliff. He had to go very slowly. When he got there, the girl was alone. She told him Eagleman had gone hunting for another person to eat but he would soon be home. She was afraid Eagleman would kill Se-eh-ha when he saw that someone was trying to save her.

When they heard the flapping of Eagleman's wings Se-eh-ha turned himself into a fly and hid with the other flies in the back of the cave.

As soon as he landed, Eagleman asked the girl, "Did someone come here? I smell a human being."

"Who could climb up here?" the girl said.

Finally Eagleman went to sleep. Then Se-eh-ha changed from a fly into the form of a strong young man. He took a rock and killed Eagleman. Then he carried the girl down the cliff and she went back to her own people.

Se-eh-ha disappeared again. That is his way. The old people say he only appears once in a while in times of great trouble. He has not come now for a long time.

Jacky Giff and Duane Allison • Pima, St. John's School

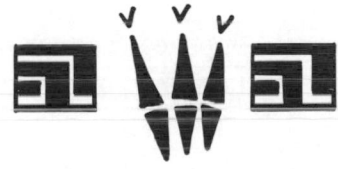

HOW THE YEI
SAVED
THE PEOPLE

On Navajo land you can still see a place where ancient animals and snakes were once killed by the giants called Yei.

At the beginning of the world one Yei carried a large clay pot with a great cruel snake in it. Once he stumbled and fell and the pot broke. The great snake got free. He would have killed everyone but the giant Yei fought a battle with that snake and killed it. The world was saved.

You can see where it happened. The earth looks torn up and strange rocks look like the hardened blood of a serpent.

Darlene Keams ● Navajo, Tuba City Boarding School

MOUNTAIN
SPIRITS

In ancient times the Mountain Spirits lived up in the high cliffs and caves of the mountains overlooking the Apache people.

They were there when the Apaches needed them. Once a great illness came upon the people and they were not able to walk. Many of them were dying.

The medicine men of the tribe called to the Mountain Spirits (or *gan)* to come down and save the people. They came in darkness and sang and danced all night long until the people were healed and could get up and walk again.

Many times after that when great troubles came to the Apaches the Mountain Spirits came down to drive away the evil.

The real Mountain Spirits do not come down from the mountains any longer. Some people say it is because they are not respected enough that they refuse to come. Many years ago the Mountain Spirits taught certain men of the Apache tribe how to dress and dance to take their place in ceremonies. Even now that knowledge is passed on and the ones who take their place also have power to bless the people.

Group story: San Carlos Apache, Rice School

THE MAZE

In ancient times Se-eh-ha, who is also Elder Brother, needed a safe place to live. He still had a lot of work to do getting the world ready for the Pima and Papago people but he could not do his work because his enemies were always following him.

Even when he went to live in a cave, his enemies followed him. They did not want him to be able to help his people.

Finally he decided to build a home underground in the center of a mountain. At the edge of the mountain anyone could see the opening that led into his house but getting there wasn't as easy as it looked.

Anyone who wanted to find Se-eh-ha had to follow many narrow winding paths that went around and around. His enemies did not know which path to take. If they chose the wrong one they got lost and ran out of air and died down there in the darkness.

While his enemies were searching for him, going around and around in all directions, Se-eh-ha was sitting safely in his cave. The only trouble was that he wanted his friends to be able to come to him without getting lost. He made a map for them and anyone who followed that map could make his way in without getting lost.

Even now the Pima and Papago Indians use that map. The women make a design of it and weave it into baskets so we never forget how to find the right path through life. It can lead you to a safe place.

Christine Manuel • Pima, St. John's School

PEOPLE CAN TURN INTO ANYTHING

Today Indian children may hear their legends sitting in the same kind of house anybody else sits in. They may hear them told the way anybody else hears a story told.

But the old people remember when the storyteller was so important that many other people would crowd around to listen— people of all ages. He knew the ancient songs that went with the stories and he would move as he spoke, maybe even dance. He used chants and special voices.

And they say that firelight seemed like a part of the stories in those days because they were always told at night and by the time the stories were ending the fire would have burned down to embers.

THE EAGLE
AND THE BOY

This happened long ago in the village of Old Oraibi.
People had eagles tied up on the roofs of their houses the same way we do now because eagles are important for ceremonies.

Just as it is now, somebody had to go up there every day to take care of the eagle and give it food and water.

So this boy long ago had to go up on the roof every morning before he went to work in the fields. He went up again in the evening before supper. He was the one who took care of the eagle.

The boy was busy with the work he had to do out in the cornfield. He was busy working with the squash and melons and beans but he took time when he fed the eagle to stay and talk to him. He always stayed up there on the roof as long as he could. Sometimes he even stayed up there after it was dark. As the summer passed, he told the eagle all his thoughts.

When he was not with the eagle he still thought about him. When he was eating supper with his family, he was very quiet. He would just sit there thinking about his eagle.

He got up when it was still dark so he could be with the eagle before he had to go to the fields, and out there working all day, he still thought of him.

Then one day instead of going to the fields when he was supposed to, he went back up to the eagle on the roof.

This is what he told the eagle: "I want to go with you to the place where eagles go when they die."

The boy untied his eagle and got on his back. They flew up into the sky above the village.

When they were flying over the cornfield where the boy's mother and father were working, the boy began to sing. It sounded like an eagle singing.

The people heard his song and looked up. They saw an eagle circling, moving higher and higher and higher until it was out of sight.

The mother and father sadly went home.

On the other side of the sky the eagle and the boy came to another world.

Alvin Kooyahoema ● Hopi, Hotevilla-Bacabe Community School

DO YOU WANT TO
TURN INTO
A RABBIT?

There was a boy who was so bad. He was always fussing. He said mean things to his mother, to his father, to his sister too. He was the worst person anywhere around.

This is what happened to him. They said, "You better go live by yourself."

He went out. He thought he'd find another place to live. And as he went out there in the desert he began to change. First he felt his ears getting longer... a lot longer. He felt his legs getting shorter... a lot shorter.

He was turning into a rabbit.

If you can't get along in a house, sometimes you turn into a rabbit. Then you live in a rabbit hole by yourself.

This boy decided to get along.

Reginald Antone • Quechan, Ft. Yuma Library

SEVEN PIMA STARS

This happened long ago at the place we call Homathee.

Seven Pima boys wanted to dance with the men in a ceremony that lasted all night. They knew children were not supposed to dance that ceremony but they didn't care. They started dancing around the fire just like the men.

The chief saw them. He told them, "Stop that. Something bad can happen if you dance when you are not allowed to."

The boys didn't listen to him. They went into the desert and built their own fire and danced around it all night long.

Suddenly ropes dropped down from the sky and caught the seven boys. Even then, they kept on dancing.

The boys were lifted into the air, dancing as they went.

They were lifted so high into the sky they turned into stars. You can see them there at night. If you look up you can count seven stars close together, dancing still.

Donald Sabori • Pima, St. John's School

LOOK UP
AT STARS

You can see the stars are like people. Sometimes you can tell which ones used to be people.

Indians know of many times that people have been changed into stars. Here is one of those times.

A man was going to die. He told his children to follow him to a mountain over there. He told them to be sure they did not look back. They couldn't help it. They looked back in the direction where they used to live, back toward their home.

At that moment the man changed into a wolf. He chased the children and he would have caught them except that suddenly they changed into stars. They rose up into the sky. That is the way they escaped from the wolf.

You can see them there.

Ricardo Juan • Pima-Papago, Ft. Yuma Library

THE BOY
WHO BECAME
A DEER

This happened long ago.

Coyote found a baby sleeping under a bush. He asked his grandmother what to do with it. She said, "Just take it to the deer. They will know how to raise that child."

Coyote did that. He carried the baby in his mouth to the place where deer lived. A mother deer took the baby and gave it milk and it lived with the deer and grew up like a deer, running with them and hiding with them in the hills.

But there was a woman in the village who kept saying, "I need a boy."

She heard about the boy who lived with the deer so she went and got him and brought him to her village.

At that time he was five or six years old, still very young.

The other children stayed close to the village on top of the *mesa*. But this boy was always wandering away. It seemed like he wanted to go back to the hills. Day after day the woman had to walk around looking for him and sometimes that made her cross.

The day came that she was busy weaving a plaque and she forgot to keep her eye on the boy. It was afternoon when she went up to the second roof of the village and looked off in all directions.

Here's what she saw. The boy was sliding on a sunbeam from one of the high roofs down to the ground.

So the woman ran back and told her husband, "He's not a human boy. He can slide on the rays of the sun."

Her husband knew that it must be true that the boy was not human. Thinking of it, they were both sad.

The boy did not come back that night though they called and looked for him.

Five days passed. Then a group of men from the village happened to go back into the hills for wood. They saw a herd of deer running past them. This boy ran with them and he made his own sound when he ran because he wore little bells tied around his ankles.

Several times after that people from the village caught a glimpse of the boy. He was always running with the deer. They heard his bells ringing.

The woman missed the boy even though she knew he was not human. So the people of the village decided to catch him for her.

All the men gathered and started the journey together. They went toward the hills where the deer live.

They found the herd of deer and sure enough the boy was with them. The men made a circle around the deer. One by one, they let each deer run out of the circle. But they would not let the boy run out. They kept him in the circle and they moved closer and closer. That is how they caught him.

They took the boy back to the village. A medicine man told them what they had to do if they wanted to make him into a human boy, not a deer.

This is what the medicine man told them to do. They must put the boy into a house which was so dark that no light from outside could get in. Any cracks in the stone walls of that house were to be plastered with more mud.

The medicine man said that no one must look in until the end of the fourth day after the sun had set. The parents would have to leave enough food in there for the boy to eat for four days because it was very important that no one open the door even a crack.

The medicine man said that if everyone did exactly as he told them, then they would have a human child, not a deer.

Everything went well through the third day. Every day they heard the sound of bells tinkling inside that dark house.

On the morning of the fourth day the woman again listened outside. She heard no bells.

She was very excited now. She wanted the boy back more than ever and since she did not hear the bells she thought surely she did not have to wait until night to open the door.

She opened the door just enough to peep in, just a little way. But the second the door opened she heard the jingle of the deer bells begin again.

The woman's husband said, "We might as well give him back to the deer."

They knew they had ruined the medicine man's cure by not doing exactly what he said. There was no hope now.

So they opened the door all the way and let the deer-boy out of the house. They sprinkled cornmeal on him for a blessing as he went bounding toward the hills.

People say that ever since then, whenever danger comes to the deer, the boy is with them, shaking and dancing and jingling his bells.

Many people tell of hearing him.

Now that boy has become a *kachina* and you can see him sometimes dancing down in the *kiva* in night dances. He is dressed with antlers on his head and he is beautiful, shaking and dancing like a deer.

Ray Masayesva • Hopi, Hotevilla-Bacabi Community School

BROTHER COYOTE

He is Brother Coyote, Trotting Coyote, Changing Coyote, Trickster Coyote. He is everybody's favorite loser. He can be killed but he always comes back to life.

Every tribe knows that Coyote was trotting around at the beginning of the world. He started his mischief before there were any people here. In fact, he tried to help make the first people out of clay but he did such a bad job they had to throw those people away and start over.

He tried to help make the world too. The stars were supposed to be put up in the sky in an orderly way, evenly spaced. But Coyote ran around and threw them and they stuck there the way they are now. That's Coyote for you.

Coyote does terrible things but he does them cleverly. He thinks of things no one else could think of, schemes to trick and cheat and fool his friends—and then he almost always gets fooled himself.

They say we learn good lessons from Coyote.

COYOTE
GETS TURKEY
UP A TREE

Coyote is a great figure for the Apaches. He is good at tricking other animals but he is always getting fooled himself. Coyote stories show our pleasure in outwitting our enemies — and they also show how easy it is to be fooled.

Here's one way Coyote was fooled.

Coyote found Turkey up in a tree.

He knew it would be easy to catch him. All he had to do was chop down the tree.

Coyote chopped and chopped. Just as the tree was about to fall, Turkey flew to another tree.

Coyote knew what to do. He got busy chopping that tree down too. He chopped and chopped. Then just as the tree was falling, Turkey flew again.

That went on all day. By evening Coyote was lying on the ground panting. Turkey just flew away home.

Tina Naiche • San Carlos Apache, Rice School

COYOTE
HAS TO HAVE
HIS WAY

Coyote met a bumblebee. Bumblebee had something in his hand.

Coyote asked him, "What do you have there, old man?"

Bumblebee said, "I don't want anybody to meddle with this."

Coyote begged Bumblebee but Bumblebee kept saying, "This is not for you."

Coyote just *had* to know. "Please tell me, good friend."

Finally Bumblebee said, "Well, all right. But you cannot see it here. You must take it home and get your family to build you a new hut and cover the hut with skins so nothing can get in or out. Do not even have an opening at the top. Then get inside and close the door and tell your family to pile rocks up all around the outside so that you cannot get out. And then open the package."

"Oh, thank you, thank you..." Coyote grabbed the package and ran all the way home. He did everything Bumblebee had said.

When he was finally inside the new hut he opened the package.

Many bumblebees flew out as soon as it was opened. They stung Coyote though he yelled for help as loud as he could. Poor Coyote.

Tina Naiche • San Carlos Apache, Rice School

IT IS NOT GOOD
TO SLEEP
ON ROCKS

Long ago Coyote and his friend, Gopher, were hunting. They stopped at a *hogan* where they found a beautiful woman sitting alone by the fire.

This woman was so beautiful they both fell in love with her. They both wanted to be close to her. Coyote pretended to be cold and said, "Woman, I am so cold, you better stay close to me." Four times he asked her that but she did not answer.

In the morning the beautiful one said, "Whoever brings back the most rabbits will be my husband."

Coyote and Gopher agreed to have a hunt. That day they rested in the hogan and when night came they sang to make it snow because it would be easier to track rabbits in snow. They knew the right songs for bringing snow.

By morning the snow was knee-high so they started out. When they were about a mile from the hogan Coyote said, "It would be better if we each went in a different direction."

Coyote started west and Gopher started east.

Gopher was a good hunter. Every time he killed a rabbit he put it on the ground beside its hole. He thought he would keep hunting for a few hours and then pick up the rabbits on the way back to the hogan.

But Coyote did not go to the west the way he said. He was following Gopher and picking up all the rabbits Gopher killed.

Gopher didn't stop hunting until the sun was sinking. When he went to pick up the rabbits they were all gone. At first he didn't know what to think but then he saw Coyote disappearing behind a hill with a cluster of rabbits on his back.

Gopher wanted to go right over there and grab the rabbits but Coyote was bigger and stronger. All Gopher could do was go back into the snow and start hunting all over again.

Coyote hurried to the hogan and put his rabbits down in front of the beautiful woman.

"Now will you marry me?"

"Not yet, " she said. "The other one hasn't come back yet so I can't count the rabbits."

They waited until very late at night before they heard a noise outside and went to look. There was Gopher smiling. He had a big pile of rabbits beside him.

The beautiful one counted them. Coyote and Gopher had exactly the same number.

The next day they hunted again. Again they had the same number.

So it went until the fourth day. That time Gopher had twice as many rabbits as Coyote.

So the beautiful woman married Gopher.

But Coyote would not give up.

He came to the hogan one day and asked Gopher, "Let's go hunting together like we used to."

So Gopher went with Coyote and they hunted for a long time. At a certain large rock Coyote said, "This is a good place to rest. You can just lie down on this rock."

Gopher lay down beside Coyote on the rock. He was very tired. He tried to stay awake but he couldn't.

As soon as Coyote saw that Gopher was sleeping he got up and stood under the rock and began to chant a spell. With that powerful chant he made the rock grow upward. It grew very high.

Gopher did not wake up until Coyote was at the end of that chant. When he looked down he was so surprised he almost fell off the rock. Far down below him he saw Coyote. It was so far down that Coyote looked small. Gopher shut his eyes and looked again... and he saw the same thing so he knew it was true.

Coyote just stood there looking up and laughing. "Good-bye, friend. I'll see you when you get down."

Gopher prayed and prayed. For three days nothing happened but on the fourth day the rock grew back to its normal size and Gopher got down and started home. But when he got to his hogan it was empty.

He built a fire and stayed there alone through the night. Before he went to sleep he put a fire stick by his side. In the morning the fire stick pointed south so Gopher knew that was the way he should walk. At sunset he came to an empty camp. He put the fire stick by his side and went to sleep.

In the morning the stick pointed west so Gopher walked west until he found another empty camp. Again he slept with the fire stick by his side.

In the morning the stick pointed north so Gopher walked north. At sunset he reached an empty camp. Again he lay down with the fire stick by his side.

On the morning of the fourth day he got up and found the stick pointing east. He walked as fast as he could. In no time he came to a newly built hogan.

He saw Coyote's children playing happily around the hogan. He saw his own children huddled at the door. They were so thin and bony he knew they were hungry.

Gopher heated up a big rock in the fire. He wrapped meat fat around it and took it to Coyote.

"My friend, if you eat this and run around the hogan four times, then when you come back you shall have my wife."

Coyote swallowed the rock. Then he ran around the hogan. The first time he ran very fast. The second time around he ran slower. The third time he began to feel dizzy. The fourth time around he fell down dead.

The beautiful woman had tears in her eyes.

Gopher said to her, "Are you crying about your husband?"

She said, "No, the brightness of the snow has made my eyes watery."

To this day Navajo grandparents tell this story. When children hear it they remember that it is not good to sleep on rocks.

Elouise Grahame ● Navajo, Tuba City Boarding School

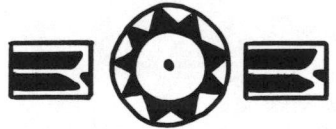

COYOTE
IN A
HAILSTORM

Coyote used to bother some crows whenever he got the chance. Once Coyote was going along when he met three crows.

"There is going to be a big hailstorm here," one of the crows said, looking up at the sky.

Coyote began to worry about the hail.

"Listen, Coyote, you better run home and get a bag and we will help you get in it so you'll be safe."

Coyote ran home and got a big bag and ran back as fast as he could.

"Now get in the bag and we'll tie it up," the crows said.

Coyote jumped right into the bag and they tied it.

Then the three crows all gathered rocks and flew up into the air and threw the rocks down on Coyote. He thought it was the worst hailstorm he'd ever been in. Coyote almost died from all those rocks falling on him.

Then finally the crows untied the bag and Coyote saw they were laughing at him. He ran away and never did come around those crows again.

Marvin Ketchum • Navajo, Tuba City Boarding School

THE
TRICKY
COYOTE

Coyote saw a buffalo killed. He knew it would make a fine feast for his family so he hurried over but a porcupine was there before him.

Coyote went up to the porcupine and said, "I saw lots of buffalo on the other side of the hill. I dragged this one over here myself but I couldn't carry any more. You can have all you want of those others."

So the porcupine went off toward the place where Coyote pointed. As soon as he was gone, Coyote picked up the buffalo and went home.

That night the poor porcupine went to bed hungry but Coyote's pups were having a feast.

William Penn ● Pima, St. John's School

COYOTE
AND THE
MONEY TREE

Coyote had some money, just a few dollars. He was walking down a road trying to figure out how to change those dollars into something more valuable.

Coming toward him were some American prospectors with their horses and mules and blankets and guns and bags of food.

Coyote had a brilliant thought. He put his money up in the branches of a tree that was growing beside the road. Then he just sat there watching the tree.

When the American prospectors rode up they asked him, "What are you doing?"

"I am watching this tree. It is very valuable," Coyote said.

"Why is it valuable? What is in that tree?" the prospectors asked.

"Money grows on that tree," Coyote said. "When I shake it money falls out."

The prospectors laughed at him so Coyote shook the tree a little and one of his dollars fell out.

Now the men were very interested. "Sell us that tree," they said.

"No," Coyote said, pretending to be angry. "This is the only tree in the world that grows money."

The prospectors said, "We will give you everything we have... our horses and mules and everything else. We will just climb down and you will own everything."

Coyote still pretended not to want to and the prospectors tried to persuade him.

But after a while Coyote let them persuade him. "All right," he said. "I will sell you the tree. There is only one thing."

"Anything at all," they said.

"See those blue mountains over there? Well, you will have to wait until I get there. If you shake the tree before that, nothing will come out and you will spoil it forever."

The prospectors agreed. So Coyote jumped on one of the horses and rode away with everything they had.

When he reached the blue mountains the men shook the tree. Only one dollar fell out though they shook and shook and shook. That was the last dollar Coyote had put there.

Over by the blue mountains Coyote was laughing.

Tina Naiche • San Carlos Apache, Rice School

HOW COYOTE
WENT
QUAIL HUNTING

There was a rabbit and a coyote. They were man and wife. They didn't have a bit of food so Coyote said, "I am going to find us some food today. Clean the pots and pans and get some wood. Be ready to cook."

The rabbit wife got everything ready but when Coyote came back he didn't have anything.

The next day he said again, "Wifey, get the pots and pans ready."

She did, but he came home with nothing.

The next day he said, "Be sure that you have everything ready. Make a fire."

But his wife said, "You've been telling me that every day."

Coyote said, "Wifey, today I have a feeling that I am going to get us something good to eat."

He went looking. Soon he saw a quail. The quail ran but Coyote was too fast for him. He caught the little quail.

Coyote said to the quail, "First I'm going to pull off all your feathers. Then I want you to go to my wife. She is ready to cook you. You follow this trail and go to my house. Tell my wife her husband sent you so she can cook you for our dinner."

He pulled out the quail's feathers. The poor quail ran down the trail, but as he was running he thought, "I don't want to be eaten. I have to think of something..."

When he got to the house he said to the rabbit wife, "Your husband said you should make me some popcorn right now."

She said, "My husband must be crazy," but she made popcorn for the quail.

Then the quail said, "Your husband also said you should make some gravy and then find one of his old shoes and cook it in the gravy for him to eat."

She said, "Now I know he must be crazy." But she did it. The quail went on his way down the road laughing and eating popcorn.

Soon Coyote came home. "Is it cooked, Wifey? Is it cooked?"

"Yes, but I don't think you're going to like it."

In those days they didn't use spoons so Coyote put one finger in the pot and licked it a couple of times. Then he put his whole hand in and came out with the shoe.

"What are you doing with my shoe?" he asked.

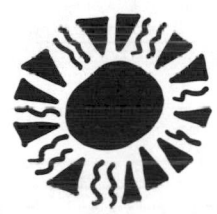

"The quail came along and said you wanted me to cook it for you so I did."

"Where did that quail go?" asked Coyote as he jumped up.

"Down the road," said the rabbit wife. "He went off eating the popcorn you said to cook for him."

Coyote ran after the quail as fast as he could. He came to a pond. He was so angry he didn't realize the quail was up in a tree eating popcorn and laughing. He just saw the quail's reflection down in the water and he thought the bird was having a swim.

"I must get him," Coyote yelled.

Coyote jumped in and tried to grab the quail. When he couldn't, he thought the quail had gone deeper underwater. Coyote ran home and got his wife and said, "Come help me! Get a blanket and your grinding stone and hurry up."

At the pond, Coyote said, "Tie me up in the blanket with your grinding stone and throw me in the water so I can go deep enough to get that quail."

"My husband must be crazy," she thought. But she did what he said. She tied him up in the blanket with the stone and threw him in the pond.

Coyote never came up again.

Veronica Thomas ● Cocopah, O.L. Carlisle School (C.I.T.E. Program)

THE
BEAUTIFUL
DREAM

Many centuries ago Maii, the Coyote, was hanging around. Coyote always liked to plan something tricky so this day he went walking with Porcupine and Brother Skunk. He was thinking as he walked along.

Ahead of them a wagon was going down the road. They saw a piece of meat fall off. They all ran for it and they all got there about the same time.

But Coyote did not want to share the meat so he said, "That's not fair."

He suggested they all race down a hill and the winner would eat the meat by himself. So that is what they did.

The race started. Porcupine curled up and rolled down the hill. He won.

"That's not fair." Coyote said.

Coyote suggested another plan. He said, "The one who dreams the most beautiful dream will eat that meat."

So that is what they planned.

Coyote and Skunk went to sleep but Porcupine stayed awake. He had a plan of his own.

Finally Coyote and Skunk woke up and told their dreams. They were both good dreams. They were both beautiful dreams.

Then they asked Porcupine what he had dreamed.

Porcupine said, "I dreamed I ate the meat."

They all jumped up and looked in the tree where they had left the meat. The meat was gone and Porcupine was looking fat.

Lana Semallie • Navajo, Tuba City Boarding School.

THERE IS MAGIC ALL AROUND US

There is magic all around us. There is power in the smallest things. It is in birds and songs. It is in sun and wind and dreams and rocks. It is in everything in nature.

These stories are all about that power— not a power that was long ago and is almost forgotten, but something that can touch us still.

WHEN
GERONIMO
SANG

There is a power in songs. Once when Geronimo was on the warpath he fixed it so that morning wouldn't come too soon. He did it by singing.

The Apaches were going to gather at a certain mountain and Geronimo didn't want it to turn light because then the enemy would see his people and know where they were going. He wanted morning to break after they had climbed over the mountain and were safe on the other side.

So Geronimo sang and the night stayed for two or three extra hours.

Group story: San Carlos Apache, Rice School

DESERT SNAKES
AND
DESERT PEOPLE

When the world started, all desert people and desert snakes lived in peace. People did not fear snakes and snakes did not fear people. They understood each other's ways and were polite to each other.

It has been known for centuries that no Yuma Indians were ever bitten by a snake unless they forgot to give the sign of friendship or showed disrespect.

Snakes and people do not understand each other now as well as they used to. But even now Indians say you should never kill a snake unless it wants to come into the hut and bite you. If you kill it for that reason then you must hang it up on a post so the other snakes will see it and understand what happened.

The snakes that pass by will say, "Look, he was bad. He had to be punished by our Indian brothers. Let us leave in peace."

Group story: Quechan, Ft. Yuma Library

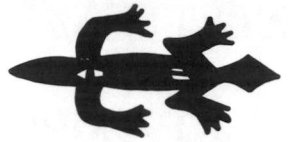

WHEN
KACHINAS
SING

Songs are used for bringing rain. The most powerful songs in the world are the ones *kachinas* sing when they dance. They can make anything happen. Their songs are from the beginning of the world and they are so old you cannot understand their language. They have never changed. That is why they are so strong.

Group story: Hopi, Second Mesa Day School

LEAVE
SNAKES
ALONE

Indians say if you bother a snake's nest and crack the eggs, then that snake will come after you and try to kill you.

Once two men were hunting and they came upon a snake's nest and one of the men said, "I'm going to crack these eggs."

The other man warned him not to but he did it anyway.

They did not know that as they left the snake was following them. It followed them all the way to their village.

When the men turned around and saw the snake they began to run. They got to their houses but they still weren't safe.

Every time they look from their houses they see that snake up on a pole looking for the killer.

Mary Penn and Bridget Shelde • Pima, St. John's School

THE POWER
OF BIRDS

Navajos know the magic things birds do for people.

There have been times when a Navajo, lost in a snowstorm with no way of finding his path back home across a mountain, has heard a bird sing.

He follows that bird and it leads him to a safe place, sometimes all the way home. It sings to him and suddenly he understands what it is saying. It saves his life, then flies away.

Group story: Navajo, Many Farms School

BE CAREFUL
OF FALLING STARS

In our tribe they say you should be very careful when you see a falling star.

You should never lift your hand and trail that star with your finger as it falls. You should never lift your hand to point in that direction.

Sometimes a grandmother will warn her granddaughter about this thing.

Once a Pima girl saw such a bright star falling. She forgot her grandmother's warning and held up her hand and trailed the path of the star with her finger.

A rattlesnake bit her that night and she almost died. When she promised her grandmother that she would remember the warning if she ever saw another falling star, she began to get better.

Donna Giff ● Pima, St. John's School

APACHES
LIVE CLOSE
TO NATURE

The Apache tribe began from the two sons of Changing Woman. The father of one of those sons was WATER and the father of the other was SUN.

Since that time everything in nature has been sacred to Apaches. We are related to water and to sun.

There is a mountain in San Carlos which is held in higher regard than any other mountian. It is called Triplets.

We are told not to climb up there and disturb anything because if a little child were to touch something there he would not grow up but would stay a child forever.

Apaches believe the balance of nature should be kept and all parts held in reverence.

Group story: San Carlos Apache, Rice School

ONE WHO HAD
THE POWER
OF OWLS

There used to be a woman who understood everything the owl said with his strange cries. She used to go outside every time the owls came and hooted for her. Sometimes they told her who was going to die in the village.

This woman had the power of owls. Once people thought she was going to die, but she told them that even though she might seem to be dead she would not be. She told them to wait four days before they had any ceremonies for her. She lay dead for three days but on the fourth day she came to life again and went on talking to owls.

After that she was a medicine woman, a doctor. She used owl feathers to heal the sick. Once some men wanted to steal her power so they stole her owl feathers from her medicine bundle and buried them by a small post.

The gray owl came to her and told her in his owl language where the feathers were and who had taken them. She understood him and went and dug her feathers up.

No one could fool that woman and after that no one tried to. They knew she had the power of owls.

Francine Redbird ● Pima, St. John's School

WE ARE KIN
TO TREES

The Great Star Man went to chop down a tree to make a shelter for his people. But before he put the axe to the tree, the tree fell down beside him.

The tree said, "Do not chop me. I am your father. You are my son."

That happened at the beginning of the world. It has happened since. Someone—always an Indian—will go to chop a tree and that tree will speak aloud and say, "Do not chop me. I am your father. You are my son."

It is true.

It is still that way.

Carla Soke and Karen Chiago • Pima, St. John's School

Byrd Baylor is the author of many distinguished books for children, among them *When Clay Sings,* illustrated by Tom Bahti, a Caldecott Honor book; *They Put on Masks,* illustrated by Jerry Ingram; *Everybody Needs a Rock,* illustrated by Peter Parnall; and *The Desert Is Theirs,* also illustrated by Peter Parnall, a Caldecott Honor book. Ms. Baylor lives in the Southwest.

The Arizona Indian children who wrote down these stories are all in Indian schools where the teachers are helping them work and learn through their own cultural heritage.